OUT OF THE NIGHT

LOLA M. SCHAEFER

ILLUSTRATED BY ROBY GILBERT

Whispering Coyote Press, Inc.
Boston

Published by Whispering Coyote Press, Inc.
480 Newbury Street, Suite 104, Danvers, MA. 01923
Copyright © 1995 by Lola M. Schaefer
Illustrations copyright © 1995 by Roby Gilbert

Printed in Singapore
10 9 8 7 6 5 4 3 2 1

Book design and production by Our House

Library of Congress Cataloging–in–Publication Data
Schaefer, Lola M., 1950–
Out of the night / written by Lola M. Schaefer : illustrated by Roby Gilbert.
p.   cm.
Summary: A child laughs at the increasing numbers of scary monsters that
appear at bedtime, until a ghoul that seems scarier than all the rest arrives.
ISBN 1–879085–91–7 : $14.95
[1. Monsters—Fiction. 2. Bedtime—Fiction. 3. Fear—Fiction.
4. Counting. 5. Stories in rhyme.] I. Gilbert, Roby, 1963– ill.
II. Title.
PZ8.3.S2890ut 1995
[E]—dc20   94–3330
                          CIP
                          AC

To Wyatt,
for your spirit and love.
                    - L.M.S.

For sk dunn
                    - R.G.

Out of the swamp
and out of the mire

Out of the mist
and out of the dew

tiptoed four witches
whose skin was blue....I chuckled!

Out of the woods
and out of the trees

marched six fat trolls
with warts on their knees....I giggled!

Out of the bushes
and out of the brier

fluttered eight black bats
who were really vampires....I snickered!

Out of the bubbles
and out of the gas

floated ten bulging ghosts
with eyeballs of glass....I smiled.

Out of the book
and out of the pages

leaped twelve wild dragons
breathing fire in stages.

I stopped reading
for the night,
pushed down the covers,
and turned off my light, when...

AND SHOOK WITH FRIGHT.

But my brother just giggled
as he said, "Good night."